Come Play In It

AN URBAN EROTICA

P. WISE

Credits

Model: Miami Millz
    IG: @MiamiMillz

Editor: Brandi Jefferson (2Cents Proofreading & Editing)

Cover/Formatting: Myself (P. Wise)

Contents

Stay Connected!

Website: PrettiWise.com
  Instagram: @CEO.Pwise
  Facebook: Author P. Wise
  Facebook Business: Authoress P. Wise
  Facebook Group: Words of the Wise (P. Wise Book Group)

Dedication

This book is dedicated to all the freaks out there, which is every single person on earth. Everyone has a wild side to them, it just takes the right person to bring it out.

Synopsis

Would you ever imagine a successful gynecologist could get wrapped up in the web of an escort? Anything is possible.

Aria "Riri" Rose was a lost soul. After being raised in the system and losing her brother at a young age, Aria turned to someone she thought would make her whole. The upbeat life he gave her of designer, luxury cars, and homes came at an expense, one she had to pay for with what was between her legs.

Silas Stevens was born into a drug family, but instead of joining the family business, he became a doctor, a gynecologist at that. He always stayed out of the way and did his own thing, but that was until he reconnected with a familiar person from his past.

While it all started with just mind-blowing sex, the two started to catch feelings. Are they compatible with the different lives they live? Would their chemistry be enough to want more and beat the odds against them?

Chapter 1

ARIA "RIRI" ROSE

"Fuckkk! Deeper baby, deeper!" Kyra howled out.

When we checked the condo out together, the realtor told us the rooms were soundproof, but clearly, it was a lie. I heard every moan, groan, and slap that was happening in her room.

"Ooohhh, I'm about to cum!" she squealed.

Covering my face and ears with my pillow, I squeezed my eyes, praying she really did hurry up and cum, along with whoever she was fucking.

Kyra was my right rib, my best friend, and my sister. We met in foster care and were raised in the same group home. We went to school together, cried together, did our dirt together, and experienced good and bad times together.

Moments later, I heard them both roar out in pleasure at the same time.

Thank God, I thought to myself.

Not only did I want the noise to end, but I was ready to pull up on her about bringing someone to the crib. The rules were strict, no men, period, but clearly, she had amnesia or just really didn't give a fuck.

I stayed in bed for a few more minutes, patiently waiting to hear the condo door open and close. After waiting a good ten minutes, I finally heard whoever he was had left. Jumping out the bed, I dashed out of my room before Kyra could even get back to hers.

"Really?" I scolded as I walked up to her.

"What?" she nonchalantly asked.

"Bitch, you know the rules. No men allowed. Shit, nobody allowed in this muthafucker."

"Riri, relax, please," Kyra called me by my nickname.

"Let Wood find out, and it's not only your ass he's going to hang, but it'll also be mine and the other girls. You acted real selfish with this one, Ky."

Wood was our Sir, the man who took care of us, the man in charge, and also our Mack.

"Fuck Wood, he ain't gon' do shit, and them bitches won't say a word because he gon' get on their asses, too." She curled her lip.

It made no sense speaking to Ky, especially when she was on her high horse and thought she was right.

"You're right." I pointed at her. "I'm finna get outta here

and go shopping before he cut our cards or some shit." I sucked my teeth, waved her off, and walked away.

As I took steps away from her, I heard her mumbling under her breath. I didn't even take it personally since she didn't say it out loud or direct. I knew I would've dragged her ass into the next day, so it didn't make sense for me to press her again.

I rushed into my room and got dressed. Throwing on a graphic crop top and short shorts, I slid my feet into my tan Yeezy's. I gathered my wallet and other necessities and dropped them in my Louie bag. Without wasting another second, I grabbed my car keys and jetted out the door before anyone asked to come along. On the way out, I shot Wood a text to follow protocol.

> Me: I'm running to the mall to pick up some stuff. I won't be long. Call me if you need anything.

Wood wanted to know our every move, when we ate, shit, slept, shopped, and especially if we were with a client or trick because he wanted his bread in the end.

Within minutes, I was in my car and pulling out of the garage. Hopping on the highway, I mashed on the gas and made my way to Christiana Mall in Delaware. Knowing Wood, if he found out what Kyra did, he was going to punish us all, and one thing he would do was lock all of our credit cards. So, some retail therapy ahead of time made the most sense at that point.

I made my rounds to the different stores, making sure to hit all my favorites: Nordstrom, H&M, Victoria's Secret, and

PINK. With every swipe, my smile grew wider and wider as my heart skipped a beat anytime the machine started to shuffle out the receipt.

Just when I was getting ready to leave, a text from Wood came in.

Wood: Bring your ass here now.

Me: Okay. On my way.

My eyes rolled into the back of my head as I hit the sent button. I just knew it was some shit popping off, and since I knew better, I hurried my ass out of the mall, into my car, and onto the highway to get home.

As I approached the door to enter the condo, I heard a bunch of commotion on the other side. My body stiffened up while my nerves started to run wild. With the keys in my hands, I inserted the house key into the keyhole with shaky hands and turned to open the door.

"Bitch, come here! You gon' learn one way or another!" Wood spat.

All I heard was his roaring voice echoing throughout the place, along with cries and pleas from Kyra and the other girls. Reluctantly, I walked further into the condo and finally reached everyone. The moment my feet entered the room, everyone turned my way.

What the fuck did I do? I thought to myself.

Kyra was on the floor crying with a bloody face while the other two girls, Trish and Rochelle, were standing there crying and looking dumb.

"What's going on?" I asked, looking confused.

I knew damn well what was going on. Somehow, some way, Wood's ass found out about Kyra bringing a nigga into our space.

"The fuck you asking like you don't know?" he jumped on me.

"What are you talking about, Wood?" I kept a firm stance as he walked up closer.

"So, you're telling me you weren't here when that stupid ass bitch brought a nigga in my spot?" he asked in a nonchalant tone.

"Nah, I wasn't."

Wap!

I tasted blood from my throbbing lip and instantly regretted trying to cover for Kyra and lied to Wood.

"I have cameras in here, so I know for a fact your ass was in here while she was fuckin' ol' dude," he confirmed.

Fuck! I cursed myself.

Knowing how Wood rolled, I should've known he would have cameras set up where we couldn't even see them. In my defense, I didn't think about it because I knew I was never doing anything I wasn't supposed to. A bitch enjoyed looking pretty and not lumped up.

"Sorry," I muttered with my head down.

"Sorry, who?" He got in my face.

"Sorry, Daddy," I corrected.

"Oh, ard." He grilled the shit out of me before finally breaking his stare and walking off.

"Cards are cut for a lil' while. No new niggas or bitches, just regular clients until I say so," he ordered.

As Wood walked to the door to leave, he stopped in his tracks. "I thought you said you went to the mall. Why the fuck you walked in here with your hands swinging?" he quizzed.

I cleared my throat.

"I saw your text was urgent, so I left the bags in the car and hurried upstairs," I explained.

"Mmm, right. Go get your shit and bring your ass back upstairs," he told me. "Oh, and wash y'all pussies properly. Y'all have a checkup tomorrow." With that being the last words he said, he finally left out the condo, and everyone was relieved.

THE FOLLOWING DAY, WE ALL GOT OURSELVES together for the doctor's appointment Wood set up. We visited the gynecologist more than the average woman due to our line of work. Wood made sure to get tests done from the clients we indulged with, but it was not an all-the-time thing. Who knew what the hell they were doing outside of fucking us. Plus, most of them had women at home, and who's to say they were faithful?

Most times, we always had sex with condoms on, but some

very needy clients of ours paid tremendous amounts of money just to feel our insides raw. When we encountered those clients, Wood would ensure we at least got blood work done, even if it was every freaking week. I didn't blame him, and I didn't complain. I was happy knowing my status on a regular basis.

"Ms. Hart?" the nurse called out.

Kyra raised from her seat, holding onto her side. From our conversation the previous night, she ran down the entire scene to tell me about what had happened before I arrived back home. She told me Wood gave her a good ass beating, kicked her repeatedly in her side, and messed her face up. The poor girl was wearing shades inside and a cap, trying to hide her bruises.

Watching her limp slowly down the hall just made me shake my head. I hated when any of us got touched by Wood, but it was always a reason behind it. And just like I told Kyra, he was going to snap out if or when he found out, which was exactly what happened.

I buried my face in my phone as I scrolled through my Instagram. Pass, pass, pass was all I did on a bunch of female pictures on my thread. Half the time, I didn't even remember following half of those hoes. When I kept scrolling, I came across a cute couple on vacation or what the culture refers to as a baecation. I felt a sting in my heart, swiping left on their photos.

Love was something I have always craved since a little girl. Love from family, from friends, and of course, as I got older, from a man. Wood always told me he loved me, but he told the other girls the same thing. I knew better than to think too much into it, though, because love was non-existent for me, especially with my lifestyle. It was just sex.

"Ms. Rose?" the nurse called out.

I snapped out of my trance and glanced up to see Kyra walking back my way.

My turn, I thought.

Getting up from my seat, I followed the nurse down the hall and into a room.

"Get undressed from the waist down, put this gown on, and you can get on the bed once you're finished," she politely instructed.

"Okay, thanks." I shot her a smile.

I did what I was told, which was nothing new to me with the number of times we had doctor's visits. The only new thing was the office we were at. Wood claimed our usual doctor was away on business, so he got us in with someone he knows. Obviously, neither the girls nor I were in any position to contest anything, so we just went.

As soon as I was undressed and had the gown on, I climbed on the examination bed and sat there patiently until someone came in. Not long after, the same nurse reentered the room and prepped me for the doctor.

"Go ahead and lie down," she instructed. "Now, put your feet here." She placed my feet on the footrests, and there I was with my legs spread open for the world to see.

Knock. Knock.

The door opened moments later.

"She's ready, doc," the nurse stated.

"Good, thanks," he responded. "Good morning, I'm Dr. Stevens, and I'll be performing your pap smear and examinations today," he introduced himself as I listened to the sound of gloves being put on.

Not saying a word, I just laid there and waited for him to get started.

He rolled his chair toward me and opened my legs wider. I heard the noise of the tools being sorted and pulled out of their packs as he touched my lady part. No matter how often I had done that examination, it was always uncomfortable.

"This will have you uneasy for a bit, but just try your best to relax," he informed me.

I felt the speculum enter inside me and immediately tensed up as usual. Balling my fist up, I tried taking deep breaths as he swabbed my insides.

"Ouch!" I screamed out.

Seconds later, I felt the tool exit out of me, and I jumped up.

"What the fu—" My words were suddenly halted.

"Aria?" he asked with squinted eyes.

"Silas? Silas Stevens?" I low-key panicked.

We just stared at each other with nothing else coming out of our mouths.

"Do you two know each other or something?" the nurse intervened.

Finally breaking our stare, we both looked at her.

"Yeah," we answered in unison.

"How long has it been?" he asked in disbelief.

"I have no clue, almost a decade, I think."

"Wow." He chuckled.

"Ummm, I'm sorry, but doc, we have a tight schedule to stay on top of," the nurse interrupted.

"Oh shit, yeah. Lay back down, Aria. Let me finish the examination."

I nodded and did what he said.

"Take a deep breath and let it out. Do as many as you need," he suggested.

I felt his fingers at my opening, and the next thing I knew, he slid them right in, and my body shivered. He made his way all the way to my spot, and I didn't know if I was trippin' or not, but it felt like he curled them, which sent waves of pleasure down my spine. I felt myself getting wet and hoped he didn't notice.

Silas finished the examination, removed his gloves, and washed his hands as I sat there just staring at him.

"It was nice seeing you, Aria," he stated, then exited the room.

"You can get dressed now," the nurse butted in once again.

Bitch, just shut up for one minute, I thought in my head to say out loud. I was in a complete trance, and I wanted Dr. Stevens to come back.

SILAS STEVENS

In my office, I sat there stuck and shocked all at once. Seeing Aria reminded me of my past as a young boy and how far I had come in life. Seeing her was both hard and refreshing. My past wasn't all great, but I knew people with much more painful memories.

Aria and I went to the same high school, where I hooped on the same basketball team as her brother, Andre. While she and I weren't actual friends, her brother and I had a solid friendship. There were times I had to step in and help her out in many situations where she was defenseless. Aria wasn't fortunate like many others. She wore the same old clothes and sneakers over and over, along with her brother and foster sister Kyra. People would make fun of them and constantly test their gangsters, but not always in a fair way.

One thing about Aria, she was undeniably beautiful, but it wasn't enough for a nigga like me to get involved with her. Plus, it was my boy sister, so I stayed in my place. Seeing her again, I realized she was even more gorgeous than she was back in the day, but when looking at her, she looked like a lost soul, and I knew why. Besides her being caught up in the lifestyle she was in, which I put two and two together when Wood sent her my way, Aria still looked lost without her brother.

Back in high school, when a group of girls was jumping Aria and Kyra, Andre and I ran out and tried to help them. Things spiraled out of control, and another kid came and pulled Andre off one of the girls he was trying to get off his sister. When the kid grabbed Andre, he flung him into the street, and a truck ran him over. He was pronounced dead on the scene, and Aria was never the same after that.

The door to my office opened, snatching me out of my thoughts.

"What are you doing?" Shanice asked with an attitude.

Shanice was one of the head nurses at my clinic.

"I'm chillin', wassup?" I looked at her.

"Chillin? Are you seriously going to finger fuck that girl in front of me? I saw the way her body responded to you," she snapped.

"And?" I raised a brow.

"And? You drawn right now. So, disrespectful."

"Are you my bitch, Shanice?"

She got quiet and just stood there looking at me.

"I thought so. But come here and suck my dick. You just stressed me out, and I need to let one off."

Shanice didn't say a word. She simply locked the door, came over, dropped to her knees, and started to pull down my scrub pants and boxers. She grabbed my tool and wrapped her pretty lips around it, making her way up and down.

Grabbing a handful of her hair, I pushed her face deeper into my lap. I wanted to feel the back of her throat. Shanice knew she fucked up by the way she approached me, so she wasn't letting up. She continued to deep-throat my shit the way I liked it.

"Spit on it," I demanded.

She rose up for a hot second and spit all over my shit. Not wasting any time, she sucked and jerked my dick at a rapid pace. I felt my nut coming, so I tightened my grip on her head and made her speed up while she took my tool in deeper.

Holding her head still while my dick was sitting at the back of her throat, I emptied my kids, ensuring she caught every bit of them.

"Oh, fuck." I sighed out loud.

Shanice looked up at me with watery eyes, smirked, and wiped her lips.

"Are you still mad at me?" she asked in a sexy tone.

"Just a little. I'll need another round of something else," I told her.

"That's not a problem." She stood to her feet.

"Go and get the next patient ready," I ordered.

Shanice quickly disappeared from my office, and I returned to the paperwork I was working on before Aria consumed my thoughts.

AFTER WRAPPING UP MY DAYS' WORK AT THE CLINIC, I reached out to my boy, Wood. I had so many questions, but some of them needed answers because they just wouldn't get out of my head.

Wood, real name Raymond Wood was one of my boys from sandbox days. He went to school with Aria, Kyra, Andre, and me, so growing up, we ran in the same circle. Even though he and I weren't really close with the girls, Wood used to be one of those people that would always have something to say to them anytime they crossed his path. He was a straight-up dickhead. While I had my own thoughts, I never allowed them to come to the tip of my tongue, especially when Aria and Kyra weren't problematic.

I pulled up to Wood's lounge he owned in South Philly after I left the clinic. Still dressed in my scrubs, I walked in that bitch like I owned it. I had mixed feelings on how to approach Wood because I felt he was on some real wild shit by having Aria and Kyra work for him after all they'd been through.

Walking past security, I entered his office without even knocking. He was sitting on the couch with his phone in his hand.

"Yo, bro," he looked up and greeted me.

Instead of going to give him a dap, I went and leaned up against his desk, crossing both my arms and my ankles.

"You good?" he asked, eyeing me up and down.

"Yeah, I'm straight. I just gotta ask you something," I blurted out.

"What's good?"

"You know I told you I don't want no parts of your business, especially with them girls. You begged me to see them since their doctor was gone, or whatever the fuck happened. Cool. But why the fuck you ain't tell me Aria and Kyra worked for you?"

He started to chuckle and shifted in his seat.

"Brah, I'm not laughing," I gritted.

"Aye, man, calm down. Didn't you just start off your statement with how you don't want parts of my business, so why are you questioning me, dawg?"

"Wood, stop playing. You know why I'm asking. Out of all the bitches in the world, you get those two? How long have they been running with you?"

"For years, nigga. Those hoes ain't no fuckin' saint, so quit trying to play captain save a hoe. They love their lives." He laughed.

Pinching the bridge of my nose, I just shook my head to refrain from leaping over to his goofy ass.

"Don't worry about them. They good, bro. And don't try to do nothing stupid, either. Leave them alone. They're mine," he asserted in a stern tone.

"Nigga, I don't want them. I just asked a question. One of

us gotta be ethical here. Anyway, I may need to see Aria again. One of her rapid tests came back abnormal. It might just be a mishap, but I'll let you know."

"Alright, just hit me."

I raised off his desk and walked out of his office without saying another word.

Wood was always the type of grimy nigga that played a lot of games growing up. He never tried no crazy shit with me, but I done seen him do so many people dirty, which is the main reason I fell back after a while. He wanted to stay in the streets while I wanted to pursue my medical degree. Nevertheless, I was a hood nigga by heart, even when I earned all my stripes to be a doctor. Yes, I spoke a certain way around certain people and acted accordingly, but let a muthafucker try me, and it would've been on.

AFTER I LEFT WOOD'S, I WENT TO THE CRIB TO unwind. I wanted some female companionship, so I decided to call over my main chick, Larissa. Some steam needed to be blown off.

"Hello?" she answered in a sweet tone.

"Wassup? What you up to?" I asked.

"Nothing. About to head out to dinner with my best friend. How about you?"

"Oh ard, cool. Never mind, then."

"What is it?"

"I wanted to see you, but it's ard. Go out with your friend," I told her, ready to hang up the phone. Begging was never something I did, so if she didn't have time for me, I was sure someone else did.

"I'm sorry. I'll make it up to you, I promise," she pleaded.

"I'll holla at you," I told her and banged the phone.

Next, I thought.

Looking through my text threads, I landed on one of my favorites names, Wynter, and sent her a quick text.

> Me: I'm free and in need of some wet wet.

I rested my phone down and started to get undressed. Before I took off the last set of clothing, my phone chimed.

> Wynter: On my way.

Now that's what a nigga's talking about, I thought.

I was a freak by nature and loved sex. My stamina for it was out of the world, and I needed someone who could always match it. With Larissa, she was a beautiful woman, had a head on her shoulders, and had her own. Her problem was she just couldn't handle me in the bedroom and wasn't always willing to please me when I wanted it.

Wynter, on the other hand, was a nasty bitch, and allowed me to do whatever I wanted with her, but she was too submissive. I still needed a woman with a backbone, and she wasn't it. In the world we live in, getting someone a hundred percent how you desired them to be just wouldn't happen. Instead, I just had a different bitch for different things until I met someone that was as close to having everything that I really wanted in a woman.

After Wynter responded, I went in the shower and handled my hygiene. I washed off the day's hard work and extracurricular activities. Once done, I got out, dried my skin, applied all I needed to, and got dressed. Cooking was out of the equation, so I ordered some Chinese for us and waited for her and the food to arrive.

ABOUT HALF AN HOUR PASSED, AND MY PHONE finally rang. The security system from my complex was requesting for Wynter to be let in. As soon as I granted her access, my phone rang again, and it was the Chinese food delivery.

Right on time, I said to myself.

I called Wynter's line.

"Yeah?" she answered.

"Grab the food from the Chinese guy that's coming in with you. I already paid for it," I informed her.

"Okay, I got you."

In the next few minutes, Wynter was at my door, ringing the bell. When I opened it, my dick jumped instantly. Wynter had on a netted crop top with her breasts showing and some tight-ass cotton shorts that showed her pussy print. She eyed me up and down with a lustful glare. I only had on a pair of shorts with no shirt on, showing off my ripped body and tattoos that covered my smooth mocha skin.

"Put the food on the counter," I told her.

In the back of my mind, I said fuck the food. I wanted Wynter right then and there.

She walked in, took off her sandals, rested the food down, and turned around to be face-to-face with me.

"Take all that shit off," I demanded.

She smirked and wasted not a second. The crop top was over her head, and the shorts, along with her thong, were on the ground. I followed suit and dropped my shorts and boxers. My dick was already standing at attention.

Without uttering a word to Wynter, she dropped to her knees and took all of me in her mouth. "Mmmm," she moaned out while sucking.

It was something about a woman enjoying the act of pleasing that turned me on ridiculously.

"Fuck," I whispered as she sped up.

The way Wynter was suctioning my dick and using both her hands to jerk it had me curling my toes. Wynter had that retarded neck and knew how to fuck.

"Hold on," I said in a husky tone.

I reached for my shorts and pulled a condom out. Slipping it on, I picked Wynter up and slid her right down on my dick.

"Shittt," she hissed.

She wrapped her arms around my neck as I held onto her under her ass cheeks. Thrusting in and out of her, I felt my lower part wet, and the next thing I knew, warm liquid was gushing out of her. If it was one thing Wynter was gon' do, she was going to cum for a nigga, and quick. Shorty was so wet it was unbelievable.

I raised her up in the air and dropped her back down on me. Continuing to do it repeatedly, she howled out in pleasure. It was a way her pussy opened up for me to touch the back, allowing all nine inches in without a problem. Her walls were snug, not too tight, and definitely not loose.

Leaning her against the counter, I let one of her legs drop to the ground while the other stayed in the air in my arms. Penetrating my way back inside her, she flung her head and upper body onto the counter. I wrapped my hand around her throat and thrust in and out as I delivered a series of fast, deep strokes. After a little, she started to fuck me back.

My climax was near, so I sped up as I squeezed her ass cheeks with force. The next thing I knew, I dove deep into her and exploded into the condom.

We both were bent over, breathing hard.

"Damn," she whispered.

"Mmmhmm," I hummed. "Take me out some food, though. A nigga's hungry."

I went and cleaned myself up, ate, and dug in her shit a few more times that night.

Chapter 3

ARIA

A week had passed, and Silas was still on my mind. I hadn't seen him in years since he had gone away to college down south. Seeing him as a successful doctor showed me he played no games and got shit done. I was definitely proud of him, but I was also yearning for him in a weird way.

As a teen, I always had a crush on Silas. He was fine as fuck, always knew how to dress, plus he was a basketball player who was on the same team as my brother Andre. We only spoke in passing, and there were times he intervened on my behalf when I had trouble with some of the bitches at school. Other than those times, we never spoke or hung out, even though I wished like hell we did.

Silas was way out of my league, and apparently, after seeing his position, I still was. The dude was a whole doctor while I sold pussy for a living. There was no way I could've gotten him. Plus, Wood wouldn't have let it happen unless he was paying some bread to get between my legs, and I wasn't speaking on his examination table. Back in the day, boys like him liked girls who were pretty, fly, and could fuck. I wasn't that at all. I barely had enough clothes to last me for a week of school, my hair was always pulled up into a raggedy ass ponytail, and I wasn't fucking nothing because those guys didn't even look my way.

Ring. Ring.

My phone started to ring, which drew my attention elsewhere. I saw it was an unknown number, so I hesitated to answer. The phone stopped ringing, but within seconds it started back up again.

"Hello?" I decided to answer.

"Hi, may I speak with Ms. Rose?" the woman asked.

"This is she. Who's speaking?"

"I'm Nurse Walters here at Dr. Steven's clinic. I'm calling to inform you that you'll have to come back for another examination. Dr. Stevens found your test was abnormal," she stated.

"When do I have to come?"

"When can you?"

"I'm free now," I told her.

"Let me check, one second," she replied before putting me on hold.

Part of me was worried about why my test came back abnormal, while the other part was thrilled to see Silas.

"Okay, if you'd like, you can come in at one o'clock," she informed me.

"That's fine. See you then, thanks."

"You're most welcome. See you."

As soon as we hung up, I shot Wood a text letting him know what was up.

> Me: The doctor's office just called. I have to go back in to do another test, something about the results being abnormal.

I looked at the time on my phone, which read ten fifty-two a.m. There was more than enough time for me to still relax, then get ready to go.

My phone vibrated with a notification.

> Wood: Yeah, he already told me. Handle that and keep me posted.

> Me: Ard, cool.

I laid back down in my bed and just relaxed until it was time for me to get up and get ready.

IT WAS TWELVE FORTY-THREE P.M. WHEN I PULLED into the parking lot of Silas clinic. I climbed out of the car and felt the summer breeze run through my loose curls. Looking in my car window, I made sure I looked good. That day I decided to look cute for my appointment, not that I thought it would move him, but at least I wouldn't have looked like the old busted-up girl from back in the day. I wore a tight-fitted white summer dress with a long jeans cardigan, Gucci slippers on my feet, and a matching Gucci bag to complete the fit. I also wore light jewelry and make-up.

After ensuring my look was still on point, I entered the clinic and checked in with the receptionist. I sat there with my right leg just shaking due to nervousness. I had no clue how this appointment would go, but I couldn't deny that I was overall intrigued.

While waiting and scrolling through my phone, I saw Kyra coming down the hall from the doctor's office. Her face was tear-soaked, and she looked like she was going through it. Finally, lifting her head, she saw me and immediately ran over.

"What's wrong, Ky?" I asked her as she rushed into my arms.

I held onto her tight because she looked so fragile and vulnerable.

She quickly picked her head up and looked around the waiting room, which was empty at the moment.

"I caught something," she revealed, then started to cry hysterically again.

"What?" I snapped. "What did you catch, and do you know from who?" I questioned.

"Gonorrhea," she admitted in a soft tone.

"Fuck," I whispered, then grabbed her back into my embrace.

When we had the high-risk clients, which were the ones that wanted skin-to-skin actions, we all always prayed we didn't catch anything. Most times, it was out of our control, but it didn't help us to not think about what if we caught something that didn't have an easy fix. We would not only be out of a job and out on the streets to fend for ourselves, but our health would've been deteriorating with one end result, death before time.

"Did they give you a shot and the treatment?" I needed to know.

"Yes, yes. I'm out for a few to make sure everything clears up, and then I'll have to come back to retest," she stated.

"Good, good. Just breathe in and breathe out. Everything will be okay." I hugged her tightly as I felt her head nod up and down.

"Ms. Rose?" the nurse called out.

Hearing my name made me nervous as hell after what Kyra disclosed. Suddenly I felt I was about to receive the same kind of news. I wouldn't have not only been hurt and upset but also embarrassed because Silas would know I was out there fucking those clowns unprotected.

"I have to go inside. When I get back home, we'll talk, okay?" I ran my hand on the side of her face.

"Okay."

We hugged one last time, and then I followed the nurse down the hall.

As usual, the nurse gave me instructions and handed me the gown. I undressed from the waist down, threw on the cloth dress, then hopped onto the bed to wait for the doctor.

Less than ten minutes later, the door opened, and Silas walked in with the same nurse from the first time. When we locked eyes, and he quickly sized me up and down, my body quivered, and I felt my nob throb. Dr. Silas Stevens was undeniably desirable, and at that point, I was willing to do anything to have a taste of him.

"Aria, how's it going?" he asked in a professional tone.

"Good, I'm just a little worried about why I'm back here," I truthfully answered.

"Well, your pap smear came back abnormal, so I wanted to redo it. Also, I received your labs back and will go over them with you."

"Okay, that's fine. Ummm, does she have to be in here?" I looked in the nurse's direction.

"Well, she's here for both your and my protection. Why, what's up?" He raised a brow.

"I just don't feel comfortable discussing my medical history and stuff with her in the room," I explained.

The nurse chuckled under her breath and rolled her eyes.

"Shanice, give us the room. I'll call you if I need you," he ordered her.

She gave me an evil stare and then exited the door.

Silas had his head down in my charts as a smirk graced my face.

Looking at him hard at work turned me on. Both his arms

were tatted with sleeves, which was obviously noticeable as he wore short-sleeved scrubs.

"Okay, so all your labs came back clean, so you're good there. We just have to redo the pap smear and examination. Is that's ard with you?" he asked, finally hearing his street side come out.

"Yeah." I nodded.

He got up from his seat, went and washed his hands, and put on gloves. As he sat back in the small chair, I laid back and propped my legs up on the rest. I heard him taking the tools out, and the next thing I knew, the speculum was at my opening.

"Deep breaths," he stated.

"Mmmhmmm," I hummed in response.

As the instrument entered me, I tensed up, but I tried to relax and stay calm so he could get a proper swab of my insides.

Moments later, I felt the speculum slide out of me, which was a total relief.

"That wasn't bad, was it?" he asked.

"Nah, it was better this time around," I giggled.

He was about to squeeze lubricant on his fingers until I stopped him.

"You won't need that," I blurted out.

His gaze shifted my way as his action was halted.

"It's like that?" He grinned.

"Yeah, it's like that."

Silas didn't mention another word. He just walked over,

positioned himself between my legs, and slid his fingers inside me.

"Mmm," I let escape my lips.

The feel of his fingers sliding in made me even wetter. He moved around and did his examination as he reached under my gown and felt different parts of my stomach. Once he was finished doing that, just like the last time, I felt his fingers curl, which made me shift my position.

"You good?" he asked.

I swallowed the lump that formed in my throat.

"Yeah," I answered.

Silas was about to slide his finger out of me until I tried my best to stop him by closing my legs. That's when we locked eyes again for a moment. I released my legs, spreading them apart again as he stood there with his fingers still inside me.

With hooded eyes and a lustful look, he pushed his way back inside me and touched my spot again. I moved in a motion that told him I approved and wanted more. He continued to work his fingers in and out of me as I moved my hips in a circle to match his rhythm. Silas then placed his thumb from his other hand onto my clit, which sent me into a frenzy.

"Ughhh," I moaned out.

He quickly placed his index finger over his lips to let me know to be quiet. I covered my mouth and leaned my head back with a light giggle.

With more pressure, he pressed down on my knob and massaged it while still finger fucking me. I started to move up and down on my own as if I were riding his dick but riding his fingers instead.

While he did his thing, he kept focusing on the prize between my legs. Not once did he look away from my pussy. He was so in tune, and it turned me on more. I had already come a few times, but I felt the big one coming, so I sped up my motion, prompting him to do the same. Within a few seconds, I juiced all over his fingers and the disposable paper underneath me as my legs trembled.

Knock. Knock.

"Are you finished? Is everything alright in there?" we heard the nurse call out from the other side of the door.

"Yeah, we're finished," Silas spoke over his shoulder, never removing his eyes from mine.

The door opened, which caused us to break our stares. Silas pulled his hands away from me, and I rose up to sit in an upward position.

"Let her get dressed and take these to the lab for me," he instructed the nurse.

The nurse's eyes shifted between Silas and me. She knew some shit went down, but of course, she won't mention it, or at least not to me.

"We'll be in contact, Ms. Rose," he stated and then walked out of the room.

She grilled me again and followed him out of the room with my sample in hand. I couldn't help but laugh.

Got 'em, bitch.

Chapter 4

SILAS

I swiftly left the examination room and went to my office. Washing my hands and my face thoroughly, I then dried and applied lotion to both. Without overthinking things, I gathered my belongings and headed for the door. I was done for the day. Besides, I needed to get out of dodge before Shanice's ass tried to press me about what she thought went on between Aria and me. I saw the way she looked and how fast she was moving to get the samples to the lab.

The moment I opened my office door to exit, there she was, standing there, reaching for the doorknob.

This girl never has no chill, I thought.

"Where are you going?" she asked after she noticed I had all my shit with me.

"I'm done for the day. I'll see you tomorrow, Shanice," I spoke sternly.

"Hold up, I—"

"I don't want to hear it, and don't follow me," I said over my shoulder.

I took a quick glance back and saw she had stopped in her tracks.

Taking advantage of the fact that she wasn't being pushy, I moved quickly around the clinic and left out the main entrance. Once outside, I took a deep breath in and let it out.

The sun was out, the breeze was blowing at the perfect pace, and I had just made someone cum. Overall, my day was going fantastic, and I couldn't complain.

It was wild how shit went down. I couldn't believe what had transpired, but I also wasn't a hundred percent shocked. The sexual tension in the room was so thick a knife could've cut it. Never had I looked at Aria that way, but she wasn't the young, bummy jawn from high school.

As I was about to get into my car, I saw Aria exiting the clinic. My eyes followed her, and oddly, she looked in my direction, then just stopped abruptly. Shyly, she lowered her head and continued to her vehicle. I dropped my stuff inside and lightly jogged over to where she was parked.

"Yo," I called out to her when I got arm's length.

"Yeah?" she answered but barely tried to make eye contact.

I observed her whole demeanor and fit. She had truly glowed up.

Digging into my pocket, I pulled out one of my business cards.

"Here, take my card. My cell is on it. Call me if you need anything, and I mean anything, Aria," I spoke in a stern tone to let her know I was serious.

She reached out and grabbed it from my hands fast as shit.

"Thanks." She shot me a shy smile and then got in her car.

I stepped back and allowed her to drive away while I stood there wondering how well business was going for them for her to have been driving a new Benz.

Shaking off my thoughts, I went to my vee, got in, and headed home, low-key hoping Aria would use my math and reach out.

ON MY WAY TO THE CRIB, LARISSA CALLED ME.

"Yo," I answered.

"Hey, baby," she cooed.

"What's good?" I asked in a nonchalant way.

It was the first time speaking to her since she ducked me the night and ended up going out with her best friend.

"Nothing. What are you up to for the rest of the day? I'd love to see you."

"I'm chillin' for the most part. You can slide through if you want," I invited.

"Okay, cool. I'll see you soon, then." We both hung up.

When I got home, I jumped right in the shower, and by the

time I got out, Larissa was calling my phone to let me know she had arrived. I allowed her access and waited for her to reach upstairs while I continued to get dressed.

Knock. Knock.

"It's open," I hollered.

I heard the door open and close.

"Where you at, baby?" she called out.

I walked out of my room and made my way to the living room to see Larissa standing there, looking beautiful as always.

Larissa was a classy, gorgeous woman. She wore designer, but the kind Caucasian people wore, not what the people of the culture wore. She was the type of bitch a nigga would wife off the back, but she lacked one of the most important things I needed in my life, a wild sex life.

I wanted to be able to get a quickie anywhere, like in a restaurant we were having dinner at, but that wouldn't have ever happened with Larissa. She would've been the type to say, "Oh no, I'm not spreading my vagina in an unsanitary place." While she didn't sex me the way I wanted, I kept her around, hoping she'd learn and adjust to my needs and wants.

"Hi, gorgeous," I greeted her with a quick peck on her cheek.

"Hello, Handsome," she sang back.

We both plopped down on the couch and got comfortable. Larissa rested her leg on mine as she reached to play with my beard.

"How was your day?" she asked.

Fire as fuck, I thought to myself.

"It was good, same ol'. How was yours?"

"Same. I gained two new clients, and I'm so excited about that," she expressed.

Larissa was a real estate agent, a successful one at that. She only had multi-million-dollar houses on her listings.

"That's wassup, you be killin' the game," I complimented.

"Yeah, yeah, whatever." She waved me off.

We continued to have small talk and agreed on a dinner spot we were going to order from. As soon as the food came, we both bussed it down like we hadn't eaten in years.

"That shit was good," I said before burping. "My fault."

We both started laughing.

I liked calm times like those, but only certain girls were allowed to even get the privilege.

Once we cleaned up, Larissa caught herself trying to cuddle up and rub on my thigh. I raised a brow and eyed her because she knew what would happen if I got all the way aroused. Against her better judgment, she continued to do so as we watched TV.

My phone chimed, alerting me of a text.

Unsaved number: Si?

Me: Who is this?

Unsaved number: It's Riri.

Who the fuck is Riri? I asked myself.

Unsaved number: I mean Aria.

I knew I wasn't bugging the fuck out. I didn't know anyone by that name. But it made sense she got a nickname after all that time. I quickly saved her number before I forgot and got to asking her who's this again in the future.

> Me: Oh, what's good? You cool?

> Aria: I want to lie and say yeah, but I'm not.

> Me: What's going on? Where you at?

> Aria: At this hotel, my client canceled, and now I'm wrecking my brain on how I'll make up money to give Wood. He don't be caring about cancelations and I don't want to get on his bad side.

"Who you texting down like that?" I heard Larissa asked, but I didn't respond.

> Me: What hotel?

> Aria: The Ritz

Boujee shit, huh, I thought.

> Me: Send me the room number. I'm on my way.

"Silas, you don't hear me talking to you?" Larissa continued.

"Huh? My fault. I gotta make a move," I informed her.

"Make a move? I thought you were free this evening?"

"I was, but now I'm not. I have to go handle something." I slid away from her grasp and got off the couch.

"Ain't this some shit," I heard Larissa mumble under her breath.

I guess she felt how I always did when she pulled some bullshit like that when all a nigga wanted to do was spend time and blow her back out.

Throwing on a Nike Tech gray sweatsuit and some Jordans on my feet, I was ready to dip.

 Aria: Room 515.

"You ready? I'm leaving now," I told Larissa as she watched me with a stunned face.

Girl, I wasn't trying to get no boring pussy from you.

THIRTY MINUTES LATER, I PULLED UP TO THE RITZ IN the city. I valet parked my car but told them to keep it close since I wasn't sure what Aria was doing. Making my way inside, I sighted the elevators, and took one up to the fifth floor. Once off, I looked at the room numbers and followed the path to where I was supposed to be headed.

"515, 515," I mumbled as I walked. "512, 513, 514, 515, there you go."

Knock. Knock.

The door opened, and there stood Aria in black lace lingerie.

The first reaction I wanted to have when I saw her was to say, damn. But, after noticing her body language and facial expression I went against it.

"Come in," she said in a low tone.

That's when I knew something was up.

As I entered the room behind her, I couldn't help myself but watch her ass. Aria was shaped nicely, but I also was able to tell she got some work done to her body. I wasn't one to judge, though. I enjoyed the sight before me.

"So, what's up?" I asked as I sat on the couch and she sat on the bed with her legs crossed Indian style.

She stayed quiet with her head down as if she were in deep thought.

"Can I ask you something?" I blurted out.

It had been on my mind since the moment I saw her to find out how she got caught up with Wood's goofy ass.

"Yeah." She looked up at me slightly.

"How the hell did you get involved with Wood?" I came right out and asked.

She let out a soft giggle and started to shake her head. "Wood's been the only person there for me for so long. Once Kyra and I were kicked out of the home when we turned eighteen and graduated high school, we ended up on the streets. One day while we were trying to steal some shit out of the store to eat, we got caught. Wood just so happened to be around and spoke to the store owner to let us go. I believe he paid him off. After that, we've been with him ever since. He clothed us, fed us, put a roof over our head, and in return, we did whatever he asked of us," she broke it down.

When Aria explained how things went, I knew exactly what happened. Wood took advantage of their predicament and used it for his own gain. I remember when he used to be one of the main people basically bullying Aria and Kyra. Who would've thought years later they would be considering him family?

Situations like Aria's happened so much in our society. Girls would come from nothing, and once a dude or even a woman dangles something nice in front of their face and fills their heads with dreams, they'd submit to them. It's fucked up, but in the end, Aria was only trying to survive, and she thought she saw a way out of pain and struggle.

"Damn, Aria," I mumbled. "And how have things been all this time being under Wood?"

"I mean, it has its ups and downs, but what situation is perfect, right? I may get my ass beat here and there, but that's when I don't follow his rules, so it's on me. I'm honestly tired of fuckin' clowns, but what can I do? I have nothing to give other than this." She looked between her legs.

It's wild that any women would think that all she had was her pussy to give away. At that point, I knew Aria was brainwashed.

"Nah, yo, that's not all you have. Did you ever want to do anything when you came out of high school?"

"Well, yeah. I wanted to go to college to study law, but who was going to pay for that? I asked Wood many times, and he kept saying that he would send me the following semester anytime I asked, but that semester never happened." She shrugged.

I just sat there and watched her, like I really took all of her in. Aria had been through hell and back but was still standing.

"It's more to life out there, Aria. You have to pull yourself out of whatever trance you're in and do your own thing. Andre wouldn't have wanted this for you," I voiced.

"What? Don't tell me what my brother would've wanted. Why are you even mentioning his name? Matter of fact, get out." She stood to her feet.

Quickly getting off the bed, she came toward me and tried to grab me to my feet, but of course, I weighed more than her and was taller. I stood up anyway, and she tried pushing me toward the door.

"Aria, chill," I told her when I got near the door.

"Nah, because you're doing too much."

I turned around, grabbed both her arms, and slammed her against the wall in one swift motion. Both of our breathing was intense as our chest caved in and out.

Face-to-face at this point, I leaned down so our lips were near each other. Her pretty, plump lips quivered as she tried to get herself under control. Touching her face, I passed my hands down to her shoulders and then her arms, making her jump.

I felt her emotions when she looked up at me and met my eyes. It was strange how we had that much chemistry and hadn't seen each other in years or never really had a solid friendship.

She leaned in and kissed my lips with her eyes closed. The moment I kissed her back, our tongues intertwined, and we started tussling with each other. It was from a soft touch to both of us aggressively touching each other's bodies and roughly kissing.

Aria pushed me but kept her hands on my sweater as she turned me around and slammed my back against the wall. Her hands went lower, and she felt for my dick. Once she found it, she stroked and squeezed it. I was already hard and waiting to get in between her legs. Both times I checked her lady part out, I got no scent. Her pussy was pretty as fuck, too. And one thing I knew for sure was she got real wet.

I grabbed her by the neck and pushed her back.

"Are you sure you want this?" I asked her.

With my hands still wrapped around her neck, she nodded best as she can to give her consent.

"Aria, I would fuck your life up," I whispered in her ear.

She snatched my hands from her neck and pushed me back onto the wall.

"I'd like to see you try." She bit her bottom lip.

That's all a nigga wanted to hear before taking it there.

I picked her up, walked over to the bed, and laid her on it. She immediately spread her legs open, exposing her well-shaven cat. As I undressed, she played with her clit and never took her eyes off mine.

"Come play in it like you did last time," she cooed.

Aria was positioned at the foot of the bed like she would be on my examination table. I got down on my knees and went between her legs. Her thong was still on, so I slid it to the side and placed my thumb on her clit. I blew, then spit on her knob as I made a circular motion with my thumb. She started to grind against my hand, matching my rhythm.

When I inserted two fingers inside her, her body shook for a few seconds as she moaned out in pleasure. Almost immediately, a waterfall started to gush out of her. By the looks of things, Aria has probably never really had someone cater to her needs in the bedroom. She was stuck on being the pleaser and not being pleased, something I was able to relate to.

"Oh, fuck, Si. Don't stop," she pleaded.

I continued to push my fingers in and out of her as she fucked my hand back. Seeing her reaction made me brick up even more.

"You have a condom?" I asked her.

She nodded and reached under the pillow for it.

With one hand still inside her, I ripped the wrapper open with my mouth and slid the condom on with my free hand.

Once I felt a huge warm stream come out of her along with a loud moan, I knew she had reached her ultimate peak, but I wasn't finished with her yet.

I stood up, stroking my dick as I watched her squirm on the bed. She was still coming down from her orgasm, which I felt was the perfect time to make my move. Her legs were still wide open, so I slid between them and plunged through her opening.

"Ooohhh!" she squealed out.

I gave her two good slow, deep strokes, and she was already clawing at my shoulders and back.

"Fuck, Si."

I slapped her arms away from me and pinned them to the bed.

"Don't move."

I raised up, pushed her thighs back toward her chest, and pounded in and out of her. She tried grabbing my arms again, but I swatted her hands away again. Wrapping my hand around her neck, I used my other hand to hold one of her legs in the air as I grind in a circular motion to feel every part of her insides. Wet was an understatement, but the most surprising thing was she felt snugged and just right for my size.

After a while, Aria got used to my dick, and she started to fuck back, which warranted me to change positions. I slid out of her and turned her over on all fours. She leaned down and threw her ass in the air for me to see her pussy from the back. The pink peeked at me. I let out a good amount of spit on my hand and palmed her pussy from the front to the back, then penetrated her without warning.

"Shiiittt," she cried.

"Take it," I demanded.

I grabbed a good amount of her hair and wrapped it around my hands while my other hand spread one of her cheeks. With her back arched like crazy, I took her straight to pound town.

Aria started to wild out and throw her ass back at me. I gripped both sides of her waist and delivered massive back shots, making her feel every pound intended.

As I felt myself reaching my climax, I sped up.

"You gon' cum for me again?" I asked her.

"Yesss, I'm about to cum," she moaned.

"Don't come until I tell you to."

I kept drilling my way in and out of her, and that's when I felt myself cumming.

"Cum for me, Aria, cum."

We both exploded at the same time. As I was emptying my clip in the condom while still inside Aria, I felt all her juices streaming down.

She dropped down on the bed and looked back at me.

"It's like that?" she smirked.

Trying to catch my breath, I chuckled.

"Yeah, it's like that."

I went into the bathroom to clean myself up. When I went back in the room to get dressed, Aria was just lying there staring into space.

"You good?" I questioned.

She jumped at my words.

"Yeah, I'm good."

As I got dressed, I continued to watch her motions. She seemed unhappy and not like she should've been after I just fucked the shit out of her.

I remembered her speaking on paying Wood his money for the client that bailed on their appointment. Being the man I was, I dug in my pocket, grabbed some cash out, and gave it to her. Before she took it, she stared at my hand, then at me.

"That's more than you should be paying," she stated.

"Aria, I'm not paying you because I fucked you. I don't pay for pussy, ma. I'm simply making sure you got what you need to give Wood and some extra for yourself," I explained.

Her eyes became watery and at that point I wasn't sure what to do or say.

"I'll holla at you," I told her before walking away to the door.

Before I fully exited the room, I stopped and looked back, feeling some kind of way. I knew her situation was not entirely my business, but somehow I felt I needed to find a way to help her. However, until I figured that out, I just left.

ARIA

S ex with Silas was out of this world. I had no idea he was huge like that or knew how to lay pipe down. Since kids, he had this way about him, that kind of big dick energy, but of course I didn't stand a chance to find out. The way he played in my pussy the first time I figured he knew what to do in the bedroom, and when it was all said and done, he confirmed my assumption.

The way he held my body and bent me into different positions sent me crazy. I was used to doing all the work and ensuring whoever I was in bed with was pleased. There were many times when I had to force myself to get wet and even pretend I was enjoying it. For mostly all my sexual encounters, I faked my orgasm because my mind would either prevent me from trying to have one or the guy was just weak.

Silas took me to another world with his stroke. The way he dug me out was painful pleasure. He knew just the right amount of pressure to apply and when it was the right time to switch positions. Not to mention, his foreplay was everything. I had only imagined if he had only used his tongue, but I was no fool. I knew it wouldn't have happened due to my occupation.

I wasn't really expecting us to do anything. My reason for reaching out was to really just get an ear. Instead, I got dick and money to pay Wood and have for myself. I wasn't sure what was running through Silas' mind, but I couldn't get him off mine.

When I reached home, I quickly made my way upstairs. All I wanted to do was lay down and relax. I knew I had to shower, but I wasn't yet ready to get Silas' scent off of me. His cologne still lingered on my body.

By the time I got home, it was already pushing midnight. I figured everyone would've either been asleep or out doing what they did best. When I walked into the condo, the place was quiet. I walked further in and when I entered the living room area, there Wood was, just sitting on the couch when I turned the lights on.

"Shit, you scared the fuck out of me." I held my chest.

I definitely wasn't expecting him to be there, especially since I didn't notice any of his rides downstairs.

"What are you scared for? Did you do something you weren't supposed to?" He eyed me.

"Nah, I just didn't know you'd be here. Wassup?"

"Where are you coming from?"

"From being with a client, what do you mean? I have your money right here." I pulled out the cash from inside my purse, making sure to leave mine back.

"Who were you with because your client for the day called and canceled?" He sat up in his seat.

I swallowed the lump that formed in my throat as I felt my heart drop to the pit of my stomach.

It doesn't make sense to lie when the truth will come out, I told myself.

"I was with Silas," I confessed.

"Silas?" He bussed out laughing hysterically. "You wasn't with no fuckin' Silas."

"I was, no cap."

"Silas fuckin' Stevens is paying for pussy now? Nah, that shit don't even sound right."

"You can ask him yourself."

Wood stood to his feet and walked over to me.

"And I will," he said in a calm tone, then snatched the money out of my hand. "Since you wanted to lie for your girl Kyra, you'll be taking on all her clients until she's back out in the field," he stated before leaving out the door.

"Ughhhrrr!" I roared.

Tears started to well in my eyes as my ears tingled. No matter how hard I tried to just make life easier for myself, it just always did the opposite.

"Riri?" I heard Kyra call out to me from down the hall.

I blinked back the tears that wanted to rush down my cheeks.

"Yeah, I'm coming," I told her.

I quickly gathered myself and went deeper into the condo and met her in the hallway. We both just embraced one another for a moment before walking into my room.

"I'm so sorry Wood's doing this to you, and it's because of me," she expressed.

"Girl, don't blame yourself for how Wood is. We both know how he could get."

As I stripped out of my clothes, Kyra got comfortable on my bed.

"Did I hear you say you fucked Silas?" She wore a smirk on her face.

"Chile, yes, you did."

We both started to clap and squeal.

"Bitch, how was it? Tell me everything."

"It was fuckin' fire, the best sex I ever had in my life, and that nigga's hung like a horse, you hear me?"

"Yesss! I'm happy for you, sis, but will he be a constant client?"

"He was never a client. Our sex session wasn't planned, and he didn't pay for it. He just gave me money to give Wood so he can stay off my back," I revealed.

"Shit, you better work your magic and keep him around."

I sat on the bed next to her.

"I mean, I'll try, but you know men like Silas won't take me seriously, and Wood wouldn't allow it. So, I'll just enjoy it while it last." I shrugged.

While I had thoughts of me actually being with Silas, they quickly disappeared from my head when I remembered the name Wood.

"Do just that. Enjoy it," Kyra encouraged.

I got quiet and just nodded my head.

"He brought up my brother," I softly admitted.

Kyra's eyes popped out of her head.

"What? Why? Are you okay?" She got closer to me and held my hand.

My brother, Andre, was my everything. We both were placed in the system when we were in middle school when our parents passed away in a drive-by shooting. When we got assigned to homes, we got separated since his home was for all boys, and mine was all girls.

We ended up going to the same high school, so we used any time we got from being in the same class, on trips, and those kinds of things to stay close. Andre's home took better care of him than the one Kyra and I were in. He had new clothes and sneakers and always kept a clean cut. Plus, he had friends that looked out for him, like Silas.

It was no secret Silas came from money. It wasn't legal money, but all money was green and bought things, right? Silas' father was a big-time drug dealer, and as far as I knew, he still was. With that lifestyle around him, I was surprised he went to school to become a doctor. That was what you called strong-willed.

Silas would always ensure Andre was good, and Andre would try his best to ensure Kyra and I were good. The love and protection of my brother was short-lived. He was taken out by a speeding truck when someone tossed him onto the road.

A group of girls started calling Kyra and me names outside the schoolyard, and after taking so much verbal abuse, I couldn't take it anymore, so I snapped. I punched the girl in her mouth, resulting in her and her friends jumping Kyra and me.

From what I remembered, Andre and Silas came out in the nick of time and saw the commotion. They tried to break it up by pulling the girls off us, but some guys wanted the fight to continue. One of the guys grabbed Andre and flung him into the street, where he was hit by a truck.

Over the years, I blamed myself for my brother's death because had I just walked away as usual, the fight wouldn't have happened, and he wouldn't have had to break it up. No one could've told me any differently. Every night I cried myself to sleep and had nightmares of images of my brother lying in the street, bloody and lifeless. I had no hope because the only true person left who loved me and protected me was gone.

"He said Andre wouldn't have wanted this life for me," I told her.

"Silas is right, baby. I know you don't want to hear it, but he wouldn't have wanted it for the both of us. Still, what were we to do?"

We hugged each other and lied on the bed, just staring into space with so much on our minds.

A week had passed, and I heard nothing from Silas, nor did I think of reaching out. I had been busy juggling both my and Kyra's clients. The best thing that happened was that most didn't even want to have sex. They either wanted to go on a date or just simply have a conversation and chill. Although Silas and I didn't speak, I couldn't get him off my mind. I kept replaying our sex session and how he played all in my pussy. The man was talented in all aspects, and I needed more of him.

After feeling a bit stressed, I booked myself a spa date to get a facial, get a massage, and get a yoni steam done, which I often did. After being relaxed and touched on, I felt a bit horny, and of course, only one person came to mind. I looked at the time and saw I had some wiggle room to play with, where Wood won't get suspicious, so I made a move.

Ring. Ring.

"Hello?" Silas answered.

"Hey, how are you?" I asked.

"I'm good. How are you?"

"I'm alright. Just thought I'd check in on you. What you up to?"

"How nice, but I'm still here at the office."

"Damn, this late?"

"Yeah, it's one of my late nights, and I'm trying to wrap some stuff up," he explained.

"Oh, okay, well. I hope you finish soon and go home to rest."

"Good lookin'."

"Bye," I said quickly and hung up.

Meanwhile, I was already on my way to his workplace when he mentioned he was still there. Since I wasn't far away, I pulled up there less than ten minutes from the time I left the spa.

When I arrived, I parked and made my way to the entrance. Through the glass door, I saw Silas and another nurse speaking at the receptionist's desk, so I walked inside. Looking up from his papers, he was surprised to see me.

"I'm sorry, but we're closed," the nurse announced.

"Oh no, she's fine," Silas told her. "That'll be all for the night. Go ahead home, and I'll see you tomorrow."

"Yes, sir." She gathered her belongings and started for the door. "Have a goodnight, guys."

"You as well," we said in unison.

Silas looked at me and didn't utter a word. He just turned around and walked down the hall to his office. I followed him, and the moment I entered his space, he slammed the door and pinned me against it. The next thing I knew, his tongue was down my throat.

"Mmm," I moaned out as he reached for my center.

I dropped my bag and started to undress myself as we continued to kiss deeply. When he leaned himself against my body, I felt his hard dick. Easing away from his lips, I squatted down and undid his pants, exposing his tool. Wasting no time, I licked it from the head down to the balls, then took all of him in my mouth.

"Oh shit," he groaned.

With one hand on the wall and the other gripping a handful of my hair, Silas guided my head up and down his dick. His girth was ridiculous. I found my mouth already hurting, but I wasn't letting up. I sucked the shit out of him. At a point, his knees started to get weak, which made me aware I was doing a good job.

"Get up," he ordered.

I stood to my feet, then he took me to his desk, bending me over it. In seconds, Silas placed a condom on him and positioned himself at my opening. Sliding in gently was out of the equation. Silas rammed his whole dick into me, making me arch my back more.

"Oh, fuckkk!" I yelped.

"This is what you came for, right?" he growled in my ear.

"Yesss," I cooed.

He delivered those dangerous back shots showing no mercy. Placing one of my legs on the desk, he dug deeper inside me. I was in complete bliss and didn't want it to end.

When I started bouncing my ass on him, he slapped me a few times, making sure it stung. Everything Silas did just turned me on to the extreme. I just wanted to get real nasty for him.

Not being able to hold it, I came all over his dick, and then my focus was on him. He continued to drill in and out of me at a fast pace. When I felt his dick throb in me, I knew he was about to reach his peak.

"Shiiit, I'm 'bout to cum," Silas announced.

I quickly pushed him back, dropped to my knees, grabbed the condom off, and took his dick back in my mouth. I sucked and stroked him at a steady pace, and eventually, I felt his warm sperm sliding down my throat. When he was completely emptied, he pulled out and slapped his dick on my lips.

"Good shiii." Silas grinned and winked at me. That's when I knew he was hooked, just like I was.

I got myself together and got ready to leave.

"I hope you have a great night," I told him before exiting his office.

Chapter 6

SILAS

When a bitch swallow and don't spit, that shit would forever turn me on. Aria was nasty, just the way I liked them. Again and again, she just kept on surprising me with something new. She had a nigga ready to scoop her up and run far away where no one could've found us.

Seeing her walk into the clinic, I was confused as to why she was there. However, after dumping my kids down her throat, I was aware of what she had up her sleeve. That move she made was bold, but it was the kind of shit I liked. Who the fuck just wanted to fuck at home in bed all the time? I wasn't that kind of nigga. I liked the wild, spontaneous shit.

After Aria left, I gathered myself and got ready to head out. I ensured everything was secured as I locked up and armed the place. When I turned around, I saw an all-black Charger pull up in front of the clinic, which I noticed afterward belonged to Wood.

Almost immediately, he hopped out the whip and walked up to me.

"Fuck is you doing here?" I questioned him, scrunching up my face.

"I should be asking you why Aria was here," he retorted.

I had a mind that was the reason for his visit, so I just chuckled.

"Why does it faze you?" I eyed him.

"Because that's my bitch, and if you want to spend time with her, it costs. But in all honesty, I don't want you seeing her anymore. I don't need her thinking anything of it. I'm the only nigga that has ever cared or loved her, and you ain't finna fuck my shit up."

"Are you serious right now, my nigga?"

"Dead ass serious."

I laughed and pinched the bridge of my nose.

"First, don't tell me what the fuck I can and cannot do. Second, if that's your bitch, then that's your bitch. Are you feeling threatened? Don't play with me, Wood. You know the power I hold. That's all I'ma say."

We had a quick stare-down until I walked away and got in my car. Not wasting any time, I placed my shit in drive and rode out of there, leaving him standing there looking like a straight-up dickhead.

SOME TIME HAD PASSED SINCE ARIA'S AND MY LAST encounter at the clinic. Just to let shit die down, I didn't reach out to her, and she didn't hit me up either. After seeing Wood all in his feelings, I had a mind that he'd probably gone behind Aria and threatened or even beat her, forbidding her to contact me.

At some point in a person's life, they will have to realize for themselves if they want to change, no one else can make them. I told myself that Aria would make it known when she was ready to really let that life go. Until then, I just fell back and tried to mind my business. No matter how much I tried pushing her out of my thoughts, though, she just plagued them.

Aria wasn't the only person in my head. Larissa was literally annoying the shit out of me with her continuous nags about going out to eat. I had been so swamped with work, and all I wanted to do when I got home was shower, eat, and rest. Larissa kept complaining about being unable to go out and accusing me of hiding her even though we weren't exclusive. So, to shut her up, I took her out to dinner.

"Hello?" Larissa answered.

"You ready? I'm outside," I informed her.

We did the whole get dressed up, and I picked her up at a

certain time kind of thing. I couldn't front, I missed going out, but work just always had the best of me.

"I'm coming out now."

I got out of the car like the gentle-nigga I was and waited for her. Moments later, she exited her house and gracefully walked to me. Of course, she looked good and on point.

"Hi, baby." She kissed my cheek.

I led her to the car, opened the door, and helped her inside. Quickly running to the driver's side, I returned behind the wheel and took off to the restaurant.

We arrived shortly after since it was no traffic and it wasn't far from Larissa's place. Stepping out, the valet took the car, and we made our way inside, where we were seated immediately due to reservations. The place was nice, and the crowd of people was upscale, just the kind of place I knew Larissa would've loved.

The server came over right away and took our drink orders. Shortly after, she returned with our drinks and took our orders for our choice of food. Larissa and I made small talk about how both of our businesses were going and how we'd like to expand. The clinic wasn't the only thing I had. I owned other businesses around the city and was a silent partner in a few.

As I was speaking about one of my newest ventures, my words got stuck in my throat when I saw a woman who looked just like Aria. At first glance, I knew it was her, but doubts started to settle in when I tried to convince myself that she wouldn't have been at a place like that. I was wrong to think of her like that because it was indeed her.

"Are you okay?" Larissa asked, pulling me from staring.

"Huh? Yeah, yeah, I'm good. I don't know why I zoned out like that," I lied.

I knew good and well what had me in a trance. It was Aria. She looked drop-dead gorgeous with her hair pulled up in a neat bun, as she wore a dress that hugged her the most proper way. Everything about her that night was dope, from her makeup to her jewelry.

Aria hadn't seen me yet, and the way she was playfully entertaining her date, I wasn't sure if she would've looked my way. I decided to shoot her a text.

> Me: Look up, gorgeous.

Staring in her direction, I saw her pull out her phone.

> Aria: Who is this?

Damn, my number ain't saved no more, I thought.

> Me: Silas.

That's when she finally looked up and scanned the room, and her eyes landed on me. At this time, Larissa was oblivious to what was going on. She just kept talking my head off, and I kept giving her short answers in between.

Aria quickly looked away and reverted her eyes to her phone.

> Aria: Sorry, Wood deleted your number from my phone, and I didn't get to memorize it.

> Me: It's fine. Are you good? You look good as fuck.

I saw a bright smile spread across her face, but she quickly tamed her actions for the man sitting in front of her.

> Aria: Thank you, so do you. I have to go, though.

That was the last text we sent to each other for a while. We both had people to entertain, but I had much rather be there with her.

THE NIGHT WENT SMOOTHLY, AS LARISSA AND I enjoyed our meals and drinks. I kept stealing glances Aria's way as she did the same back. I watched how she smiled and covered her mouth as she giggled or laughed. Everything about her was authentic and not forced.

When I saw her get out of her seat, I knew she was heading to the bathroom, so I did the same.

"Excuse me, I'm going to the men's room and then have to make an important call," I told Larissa.

"Sure, I'll be right here. Take your time," she stated.

I didn't want to be too far behind, so I got out of my seat

quickly and damn near did a light jog to the restroom area. Right as I made it, I saw Aria step into the room. Before I followed in, I took a look around to make sure no one was paying attention, and then I slid inside.

The moment I was near her, I grabbed her arm and pushed her inside the last stall. I was unaware if anyone else was in the bathroom at the time, but I really didn't care.

"Si, what are you do—"

I cut her sentence off with a wet-ass kiss.

"Turn around," I demanded.

She did as she was told.

I placed her hands on the walls and went underneath her dress, pulling down her thong. Sniffing it, I tucked it in my pocket and undid my pants. Quickly slipping on a condom, I wasted not another second and slid right into her hole with ease as she was already wet.

"Mmm," she moaned.

I covered her mouth with one of my hands as I used the next to grip her waist. She lifted her leg and placed her foot on the toilet bowl, giving me more way to get deeper inside her.

As I thrust in and out, she threw her ass my way, and I caught it each time. I knew we were short on time and had to make it quick, so I sped up and bent her over more so I was able to feel all up in her love tunnel.

Aria tightened her grip on my hand that she was holding, and I felt her walls contracting, which let me know she was cumming. Shortly after, I was about to reach my climax, and surprisingly, she came again, right with me.

"Oh shit," I huffed.

She turned around and covered my mouth as she laughed.

I tossed the condom in the toilet as she wiped herself clean. Before leaving the stall, she grabbed my face and kissed me deeply. With no other words exchanged, she left out.

After a few minutes, I snuck out of the women's restroom and made my way back to my table where Larissa was. Thankfully, she was normal and didn't ask questions.

Feeling mischievous, I shot Aria a text.

> Me: Stick your finger in it and taste yourself.

I looked over to see her reaction, which was a devilish smirk. She leaned over toward the table and slipped her hand between her legs. Seconds later, she stuck her finger in her mouth and sucked it dry.

That's my girl, I thought.

After messing with her a few more times, I decided to let her be, as I still had Larissa in front of me. We ordered dessert and continued to talk about everything she wanted to talk about, but after a while, I was becoming drained by her words.

"You ready, hun?" I blurted out and asked.

"Ah, yeah, we can leave," she agreed.

It's funny how things worked. When I looked over at Aria, she and her old man of a date were getting up as well to what I assumed to leave. They were closer to the door, so they made it out before Larissa and I did.

As we waited for the valet, I overheard their conversation since they weren't too far away.

"I watched you all night on that damn phone and eyeing that man. I paid for your attention, not him," the man growled.

"What are you talking about?" she acted confused.

"Did you go in the bathroom to fuck him? Let me smell your pussy."

"What? Why are you so loud and asking me that kind of shit out here?" she fought back.

"Bitch, who the fuck are you talking to, huh?"

The next thing I knew, I saw the man backhanding Aria and then wrapping his hand around her throat.

My killer and protective instincts kicked in, and I leaped over there and snatched his ass off her, landing a good punch to his mouth. I wanted to continuously pounce on his face, but I knew better. I wasn't trying to catch a case over no corny-ass old head.

"Si," Aria called out.

"See, I knew it. I'm about to call Wood right now. This is some bullshit," the guy stated as he held his mouth and walked away.

"You okay?" I examined her.

She nodded as tears started to fall.

"What's going on, Silas? And who's this?" Larissa caught herself poking her way through the situation.

"Not now, Larissa. Give me a minute." I waved her off.

"It's fine, Si, go be with your date. I'm good," Aria tried to convince me.

"Did you drive here?"

She nodded as she held her neck.

"Look, here's my car." She pointed at it when the valet pulled up.

I helped her inside, ensured she was safe, and watched her drive off. Still, the unsettling feeling that night was what would happen when she reached back home.

ARIA

I don't know what I had gotten myself into, but some shit was about to pop off. Knowing how Wood could get, I was literally scared for my life to go back home. The guy I was on a date with, Tim, made it clear he would contact Wood. I knew it wasn't a bluff either because Silas hit his ass one good time in his mouth.

As I drove back to the condo, I contemplated if I should grab what I could take, along with the stash I had been saving up, and run. I was tired of my current life and the fear that came with it being under Wood. In the beginning, it wasn't so bad. He treated us really well, but over time we saw his true colors.

When I got about ten minutes out, Wood called me, but I refused to answer. He then continued to call back-to-back times for about ten times straight. Once he saw I wasn't responding, he started texting down my phone.

> Wood: Bitch!

> Wood: I'ma fuckin' kill you.

> Wood: Didn't I tell your goofy ass to stay away from that nigga? Now he's fuckin' up my money?

> Wood: Aria, answer the fuckin' phone.

> Wood: Watch when I see you!

It was threat after threat after threat. The crazy part was that I knew Wood would live up to all of them, but I was tired of being a punching bag and someone he could drag all around the place. That's when I decided it was time I made my exit.

I mashed on the gas so I could've hurried home and done what I had to do before Wood showed up. The other girls and I never knew his whereabouts, and he'd just pop up to the house and even places unannounced. I just prayed he was out deep in Philly somewhere, so I could've had time to at least grab my stash and go.

When I pulled up to the crib, I didn't spot any of his cars, which gave me hope. I jumped out of the car and raced upstairs at the speed of light. My body was shaking as my nerves were getting out of control, but I continued to talk to myself to see my mission through.

Opening the door, as usual, it was quiet and dark since it

was a late night. I quickly closed the door behind me and made my way inside, but I only got a few steps in and was knocked down by a heavy ass blow. Howling out in pain, I was silenced with another hit to my mouth. Instantly, I curled up and covered my face.

"Wood, please," I begged.

"Bitch, shut up!" he roared.

He kicked me all over my body as well as stomped me good. The abuse went on for what felt like forever. I was able to hear the girls in the back crying and begging him to stop, but it went on deaf ears. Wood was out for blood, and no one was there to stop him.

As he continued to beat me with his fist and feet, I silently prayed for God to help me get away, get away from it all. After a while, he stopped, and I heard him wheezing. The next thing I knew, a large object was brought down on my head, and everything went black.

Beep. Beep. Beep.

I opened my eyes, and still, I saw darkness. My thoughts were I had made it to hell, where there wasn't any light. As I tried to move, sharp pains shot throughout my entire body like waves.

"Oowww!" I cried out.

"Aria, you're awake," I heard a familiar voice.

That's when I knew I wasn't in hell, and I was very much

still alive, but why wasn't I able to see? *Did that nigga make me blind?* I thought.

"Hold on, I got you," the person said.

Moments later, something was removed from my eyes, and I was able to see. Blurry at first, but my sight was coming back to normal. Blinking until my vision was clear, I saw Silas standing beside me. I looked around and saw that I was in the hospital.

"What happened? How long have I been here?" I questioned. The last thing I remembered was getting my ass beat by Wood.

"You were brought to the hospital unconscious. You suffered a few fractured ribs, bad bruising all over, and a severe concussion. Hence the reason your eyes were covered and the lights in here are off. You've been here for three days now," he explained.

"How are you here?" I was confused for sure on that part.

"After Wood did whatever he did to you, he left you for dead. Kyra called me off your phone and told me what happened. I instructed her on what to do and met her at the hospital."

Thank God she knew my password, I thought.

"Thanks for being here. You don't have to be."

"I do, and I will make sure you're good, but that's only if you make your mind up to leave Wood and that life behind, Aria," he sternly voiced.

"That was my plan that night. I was going home to get my stash and some other important things and run. I was hoping

Wood wasn't at the condo yet, but obviously, he beat me there."

"Are you sure you want out?" Silas repeated.

"Yes, I'm positive."

"Ard, I'll handle it."

"What do you mean?" I tried to sit up.

"Relax and don't worry about it. My main concern is you getting back healthy."

I nodded and felt tears threatening to escape. Silas' words sounded so genuine, and to know someone cared about me besides Kyra was a foreign feeling but a feeling I liked.

DAYS HAD PASSED, AND SILAS WAS AT MY BEDSIDE most days. The only time he left was to handle some patients, shower, and he would be right back to the hospital. He showed me the whole time how he really cared about my well-being. While around, he'd speak with the nurses and doctors about my condition and stay up-to-date with everything.

"The doctor said you improved tremendously, and he's going to discharge you," Silas informed me.

"Seriously? When?" I inquired.

"I believe tomorrow. I'm waiting for him to confirm. Are you ready to get out of here?"

"Am I? I'm over this place."

"I just want you to get better so I can hurt your insides," Silas came close and whispered in my ear.

I felt my pearl throb instantly at the sound of his sexy ass voice and the words that came out of his mouth.

"Shit, I ain't gotta move for you to still play in it." I bit my bottom lip.

"I bet."

We both started laughing.

"I have to go and handle something before you get released, but I'll be back later, ard?"

"Okay, just be careful and come back," I pleaded.

Deep down inside, I knew that something had to do with Wood. I trusted Silas' instincts. Besides, I was laid up in a hospital bed, so there was nothing I could do to stop him.

My thoughts just drifted off to what will happen next. What would've come out of my and Silas' situation? So many thoughts and questions bounced around inside my head it started to hurt. I just said a silent prayer that God sees me through everything, and he revealed what he wanted me to do.

SILAS

When I left the hospital, I had one thing on my mind, and that was to put an end to Aria's past. The situation was sticky and could've easily blown up to be something big. Before it got to that point, I knew the person I had to step to in order to get the green light to end all the bullshit.

I pulled up to my destination and hopped out of the whip. Entering the restaurant, I head straight for the back. Security was posted up as usual. As I was moving past them, one new kid reached his hand out to stop me.

"Everybody gets searched, bull," he stated with confidence.

I swatted his hand away from me, but before I could say a word, one of the regular guards stepped in.

"Nah, he's good." He shot me a head nod. "Never approach him or try to search him," I heard him tell the newbie.

I continued into the door they were guarding, which was an office. Once inside, just the man I went to see was lounging on his couch.

"Son, what are you doing here?" He stood up and dapped me up.

"What's the word, pops?"

Yes, the person who I had to holla at was my father, the OG around the city. Everything had to pass through him.

"I need to rap to you about something," I relayed.

"What, you want to join the family business now?" he joked.

My pops was a big-time drug pusher and ran all the streets from Philly, Jersey, Delaware, and some of Maryland. Growing up, he tried grooming me to join him, but I just wasn't into it. I took all the lessons he taught me and applied them to my studies. I was a hood nigga by heart, but I just chose a different way to run my bag up.

"Nah, man. On a serious note, that nigga Wood, he needs to fall back off someone I know, someone you know too," I blurted out.

"Who?" He raised a brow.

"Aria, Andre's sister."

"Our Andre that died when y'all was in high school?"

"Yeah, him. Aria has been working for Wood for some time

now. The nigga is beating on her and the other girls, but that ain't my problem. My focus is on her. She laid up in the hospital as we speak. She wants out."

"Wood's doing them jawns like that?"

"Yeah, it's nasty with him, pops. Before I lay his ass down, I wanted to come holla at you and see if you'd back me. All I really have to do is threaten him that I'll have you stop supplying him, and he won't be allowed to sell shit in this city or anywhere near it."

My pops sat back in his seat and started thinking.

"Listen, whatever you want, you got it." He threw his hands in the air as if he were surrendering.

I went over to dap him up.

"My guy." I smiled.

I knew my father would side with me. We had a tight relationship despite our different lifestyles. One thing my father and his organization didn't do was play about me. Plus, I knew hearing about Aria's predicament probably tugged at the bit of heart he had left. Either way, it was a win. The only thing left to do was to pull up on Wood and let him know the deal.

After I left my pops, I went back to the hospital to check on Aria. The doctor gave the official green light for her to be discharged, so I had to put things in place. I made Aria reach out to Kyra and tell her she was being released and to relay the message to Wood. That way, when we went to her spot to gather her belongings, it was a chance he'd be there, and that's exactly what I wanted.

When visiting hours were up, I left from Aira's bedside, but it was only for a couple of hours. I went home and got one of my guest rooms situated for her so that she'd be comfortable when she got there. My plans were to just get her from the hospital, go to her spot, get her things, and then take her right to my place.

THE FOLLOWING MORNING, I WOKE UP BRIGHT AND early. I conducted my usual routine, where I had some coffee, handled my hygiene, prayed, and meditated. I knew the day would be unpredictable, but I prepared myself in all aspects for anything to go down. Once I was ready to start my day, I went ahead and made my way to the hospital to pick up Aria.

I walked onto the hospital floor she was staying on and reached her room. However, the bed was empty. Panic started to set in that somehow Wood came and got to her before I did since we had Kyra relay the message. Searching the entire room, including the bathroom, it was no sign of her. Guilt and worry started to pass through my mind.

"Fuck!" I snapped out loud.

The nurse walked in as I was pacing the floor.

"Are you okay, sir?" she asked.

"No, I fucked up," I replied, but not directly to her.

"Heyyy, Ms. Rose, how was your walk?" the nurse asked.

I turned around and saw Aria slowly walking into the room, and all the anxiety that had built up immediately melted away.

Thank God, I thought.

Two nurses helped her get back settled into her bed as I looked on, then quickly left the room.

"Are you okay?" Aria asked.

"Yeah, I came in here and didn't see you, so I thought Wood got here before I did," I confessed.

Aria started to laugh but then just suddenly stopped. "Awwwhhh, you were worried about lil' ol' me?" She pouted her lips out.

"Man, whatever. Are you ready to go? I bought some clothes for you to just throw on for the time being." I handed her the bag I brought with some things.

"Thank you," she replied with sincerity.

"No problem. Now come one so we can get out of here."

She slid off the bed, took the bag, and went into the bathroom to get herself together. While waiting, I went through some work emails and responded to urgent matters.

ABOUT HALF AN HOUR LATER, ARIA CAME OUT OF THE bathroom looking like a whole dude. She threw her hair up in a messy bun as the t-shirt and sweats I gave her swallowed her body.

"I'm ready," she announced and flopped her hands down to her side.

I just laughed at her and stood to my feet.

"Ard, let's go." I reached out for her hand, and she took it.

We walked out and headed to the nurses' station to pick up her discharge papers. Following that, I made sure to pick up whatever medication that was prescribed to her at the hospital's pharmacy.

We got in the car, and I started driving toward her spot. After she gave directions, I noticed she kept shifting in her seat. I could tell she was uneasy about going there and more so worried about how things would go down. To comfort her a little, I reached over and grabbed her hand and just held onto it as I stirred the wheel with my left hand.

We arrived at her complex shortly after, and I found a park. I reached over to the glove compartment and took my Glock out, checked the clip, and tucked it into my waistband. When I got out, I rushed to Aria's side to help her out of the car. At a moderate pace, we walked over and entered the building. I noticed the people at the desk eyeing Aria in a kind of way, but then I remembered they must've been there or heard about her incident with Wood.

Getting on the elevator, we rode up to her floor and got out. As we walked up to the condo door, she just stood there and stared at it for a moment. Aria took a deep breath and let it out before knocking. We waited for a few seconds before the door was opened by Kyra, but instead of her letting us in, she tried to slam the door in our faces.

"Who is it?" I heard Wood ask.

Kyra stood there frozen, unable to process what was happening. We could tell she was frightened and wanted us just to leave and come back another time, but Wood being there was in my plan all along.

"Kyra, it's cool," I assured her.

She nodded and stepped aside.

We walked inside and saw Wood sitting on one of the bar stools in the kitchen, drinking.

"Oh, y'all got some muthafuckin' nerves," he gritted.

I looked at Aria to give her some reassurance that I had her.

"Go and pack your things," I instructed her. "And don't come out until I tell you to."

"Nigga, are you serious? How are you spitting out demands in my crib?" Wood interjected.

"Go," I raised my voice at Aria, and she took off to her room with Kyra behind her.

I turned my attention to Wood, who was standing at that point.

"Didn't I specifically ask you to stay the fuck away from her? Not only did you not grant me my wishes, but you fucked my paper up, Silas," Wood voiced.

"Wood, on some real shit, I ain't tryna hear none of that. You getting a whole lot of paper elsewhere. I don't know why you just don't leave these girls alone."

"I'm all they have, man," he tried to reason.

"Nah, Aria got me," I countered in a matter-of-fact tone.

Wood started to laugh hysterically.

"Nigga, what do you want with a hoe like her? She ain't got shit to offer you but pussy."

"Leave me to worry about that."

"Nah, it won't happen because she ain't going nowhere over my dead body!" he spat.

"I mean, if it got to be that way, then ard." I pulled out my Glock.

"Whoaaa, you for real finna shoot me over a bitch?" he asked, scrunching up his face.

"Nah, I won't even waste a bullet on your goofy ass." I took a few steps closer to him. "But this is how shit gon' go. Aria is leaving with me. You are not to contact her anymore, and if you ever see her out, you better look and walk in the opposite direction," I demanded.

"Or else what, Dr. Stevens?" he taunted.

"Or else you won't move not an ounce of fuckin' product in this city or anywhere near, and that's a muthafuckin' promise," I grilled.

Wood's whole demeanor softened as he took a few steps back and sat back on the bar stool.

"Aria!" I shouted.

Seconds later, she came walking down the hall with two suitcases and a bag.

"Let's go," I told her as I helped her with some of her things.

As we were leaving out, I turned and looked at Wood.

"We good?" I asked.

He raised the glass he was drinking in the air.

"We good," he confirmed.

Aria and I walked out of there, not even looking over our shoulders. I knew Wood wasn't gon' jump. He knew better. My father would've not only cut him off but killed his ass, too, if I hadn't done it.

It was not only a new start for Aria but one for me as well. None of what went down was planned, from us reconnecting to me getting her out of that wild lifestyle. Our journey ahead was unclear, but I knew we'd figure it out and do it together.

Epilogue

ARIA

Two Months Later

Silas and I had just finished eating brunch at this dope restaurant in the city. I was able to get him to leave work for a lunch break, which he hated to do so much. As we were heading out, he told me he had to make a stop before dropping me off. It was just like any other day when I did errands with him.

We pulled up to a parking garage and parked. I looked over at him to see if I was getting out or waiting inside the truck.

"Come on," he instructed.

I didn't even ask questions. I just climbed out of the passenger seat and followed him to the elevator. We took it downstairs and into a building that made us exit into a courtyard. Looking around, I saw we were on Temple University's campus. We continued to walk until we reached another building and entered. We then stood in line for approximately five minutes before we reached the table.

"Hello, good afternoon. Your last name, please?" the woman requested.

I had no idea what we were doing there, so I just stood still and listened.

"Rose, please," Silas replied.

My eyes popped open, and I looked at him because why in the hell did he say my last name?

The lady gave my name to someone else, who then started searching through a file cabinet.

"What's going on, Si?" I asked in a hushed tone.

The person then handed two folders to the lady at the desk.

"Here you go. Inside is your fall class schedule and welcome packet," she announced as she handed over the folders.

"What? No, no, no." I started to tear up.

I was in utter shock and couldn't even process what was happening. Silas took the folders as I stood there with my mouth ajar.

"You didn't—"

"Shhh." He placed his finger on my lips. "Come on."

Silas took my hand, and we left the building, headed back to the garage, and into the truck. The whole way, I didn't say a word. I was literally speechless.

"I just wanted to surprise you with something you really wanted to do," Silas stated.

I leaned over and undid his pants, having him lift up so they could drop to the floor of the car. Wrapping my lips around his dick, he jumped slightly at the touch of my wet tongue. Going up and down, I found a good rhythm that satisfied him and me.

Silas started to massage my ass, which was in the air, then found his way under my dress and thong. With this simple touch, I started to get turned on and wet. He cupped and rubbed my whole pussy, which sent me into a crazy zone, causing me to bob faster.

"Mmm," I moaned.

"Deep throat that shit," he hissed.

I went all the way down and made his head touch the back of my throat, passing the uvula. Some of his pre-cum coated my mouth, and it tasted so good. As he plunged his finger inside me, I came up for a quick second to get air and moaned out loud. I didn't care who heard or saw us in the parking garage.

"Come sit on it," he commanded.

Without hesitation, I slipped over on his side as he pushed the seat back and slid right down on his dick.

"Fuckkk!" I cried out.

No matter how many times we fucked, the moment Silas entered me, I always felt like it was the first time. Both my feet were planted on the seat as I bounced up and down on him. He had both my ass cheeks spread wide apart, gaining him full access to my insides. I rode that man as if my life depended on it. I wanted him to feel all of me.

"Damn, this shit feels good," he groaned.

"Baby, deeper!" I begged.

Silas gripped my ass tight and thrusted upward as I slammed down on him. My pussy was crying from the pain, but it felt so good. I was reaching my peak as I felt his dick throb. Within seconds, we both came. I creamed all over him as he shot his kids in me.

EVER SINCE SILA TOOK ME AWAY FROM THE WILD lifestyle I was living, I felt so much better about myself. We spoke and got an understanding of each other's past and what we wanted to do in the future. He literally changed my life for the better in all aspects. Silas told me from the jump about how he operated with women and explained to me about his main chick, Larissa. However, after we spoke and decided to give us a shot, he cut all ties with Larissa and anyone else he was having relations with, including the nurse Shanice at his office.

As for Kyra, we didn't totally leave her behind. Silas had to set up a place for her before getting her from under Wood. It was hard at first because Kyra didn't want to leave him. She was still stuck believing he loved her and that he was all she had. After many attempts and persuading Silas and I finally got her away from Wood, which of course, Silas didn't have any issues with that. So, while I was living my best new life, I was helping my best friend adjust to her new life as well.

Once he placed a stamp on me as his, Sila ran several thorough tests to ensure I was clean and free from my past. Not to mention, once he was comfortable with the results, that man played in my pussy day in and day out. He ate me up for breakfast, brunch, and dinner, and I did the same to him. Who would've thought we were going to end up together? We never know what life, or should I say, God, has in store for us. I knew my brother was finally looking down at me with a big smile.

Life with Dr. Silas Stevens was filled with love, respect, and plenty of SEX.

About the Author

P. Wise (Pretti Wise) is a National and International Best Selling author of fiction literature, whose experiences and imagination have shaped her to write about her ideas. She is originally from Trinidad and Tobago but grew up in Bed-Stuy, Brooklyn; also spent a great deal of time in Philadelphia and Chester.

Having experienced and witnessed different events in her

life, she has a variety of perspectives that almost any and everyone can understand. The love to write stemmed from a young age, as she enjoyed essay writing and penning her journal.

Coming from a lower-class family, she's a first-generation college graduate, but also, the first to enter and survive a federal prison sentence. With ambition, intelligence, and absurdly high tenacity, she'll have her place in the fiction game.

P. Wise has a 2 year old daughter, who's her world and reason for her grind.

This is P.Wise's ninetieth book since starting her career in January 2022.

Stay Connected!

Website/Mailing List: PrettiWise.com
    Instagram: @CEO.Pwise
    Facebook: Author P. Wise
    Facebook Business: Authoress P. Wise
    Facebook Group: Words of the Wise (P. Wise Book Group)

Also by P. Wise

Heir to the Plug's Throne

Heir to the Plug's Throne 2

Gorgeous Gangstas

Gorgeous Gangstas 2

Luchiano Mob Ties: Snatched Up by a Don Spin-Off

Snatched Up by a Don: A BBW Love Story

Snatched Up by a Don: A BBW Love Story 2

Snatched Up by a Don: A BBW Love Story 3

A Saint Luv'n A Savage: A Philly Love Story

Luv'n a Philly Boss: A Saint Luv'n a Savage Spin-off

Kwon: Clone of a Savage

Kwon: Clone of a Savage 2

Welcome to Cherrieville: Bitter & Sweet

Summer Luvin' with a NY Baller

Tamia & Tytus: A Toxic Love Affair

Diary of a Brooklyn Girl

Sex, Scams, & Brisks

Sex, Scams, & Brisks 2

Coming Soon

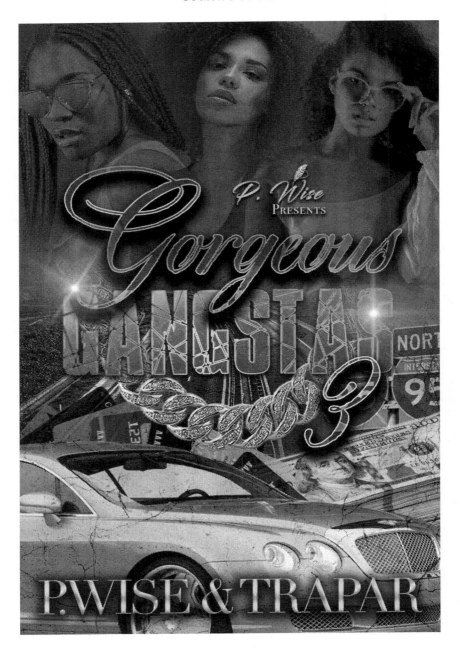

Made in the USA
Middletown, DE
28 June 2023

34102406R00060